SABAN'S

MIGHTY MORPHIN POWER RANGERS™

SCRAPBOOK

Nancy E. Krulik

SCHOLASTIC INC.
New York Toronto London Auckland Sydney

ISBN 0-590-48853-8

Book design by Nancy Levin Kipnis

12 11 10 9 8 7 6 5 4 3 2 1   4 5 6 7 8 9/9

Printed in the U.S.A.   09

First Scholastic printing, September 1994

Greetings, earthlings. I am Zordon, speaking to you from deep within the Command Center. I bring a most unfortunate message. The earth, as you know it, is in grave danger. Rita Repulsa, Empress of Evil, is involved in a ruthless quest to rule the earth. She will stop at nothing to achieve her goal. But do not be afraid. I am certain that a group of young warriors will defeat her. These young freedom fighters are known as the Mighty Morphin Power Rangers!

The Power Rangers are typical high school students. . .

. . . until they are summoned to protect
the earth. That is when they become the

Mighty Morphin Power Rangers!

They're coming to save the world!

Each Power Ranger has a remarkable talent. Jason is a natural-born leader. That is why I have selected him to lead the Power Rangers in battle and to pilot the mighty Megazord.

6

Jason fights as the powerful Red Ranger! His black belt in karate serves him well. But when he requires extra fighting power, I have provided him with the sharp and accurate Power Sword. Like all the Power Rangers, Jason draws his super morphing power from an ancient dinosaur. In Jason's case, that creature is the Tyrannosaurus Rex.

Kimberly is a remarkable gymnast. In fact, she is the city champion of Angel Grove, California. Her talent is very desirable in a young super hero.

And when she fights, her mind is solely on the battle. Rita Repulsa should fear Kimberly, the Pink Ranger, especially when she aims her Power Bow. Kimberly draws her strength from the Pterodactyl.

Trini is very kind and patient. She has a peaceful soul, but she is not afraid to fight for what is right.

When she morphs into the Yellow Ranger, Trini calls upon the Saber-toothed Tiger. Her hands move like lightning, and with the help of her Power Daggers, this freedom fighter easily defeats her opponents.

Zack loves music and dance. And, like Kimberly, he is a remarkable gymnast. It would be unwise for his opponents to underestimate Zack's knowledge of the ancient martial arts.

Zack has combined his love of music, dance, and martial arts to create his own battle style — Hip Hop Kido! And when that is not enough, Zack draws power from the Mastodon to become the Black Ranger, controller of the Power Axe.

But there is more to the Power Rangers than muscle. No battle can be won without brilliant planning. Billy is the most intelligent teenager I have ever known.

Although Billy is the brains behind the Power Rangers, as the Blue Ranger, he is a worthy fighting opponent. Billy is quite skilled in the use of his Power Lance. When it is time to do battle, Billy draws his power from the Triceratops.

Oh, I almost forgot to introduce someone very special — a most important member of our team of honorable fighters. This is Alpha 5, my robot assistant, and a friend to the Mighty Morphin Power Rangers. He worries a great deal, but only because he cares so much about our young heroes.

Rita Repulsa, the Mistress of Mayhem, launches her tirades from her fortress on the moon. She is extremely powerful. Rita and I have battled over the universe for 2,000 years — give or take a week. During that time, whole planets were destroyed.

It was Rita who trapped me in this time warp. Now, I can only speak to my Power Rangers through an interdimensional communication device. But Rita does not fight her battles alone. I can tell that Squatt, one of her soldiers, is planning something right now!

17

Rita has her own committee of evildoers. Goldar is a cold, calculating winged warrior, and Rita's favorite soldier. Squatt is a horrid creature, half-warthog and half-blueberry!

Rita's soldiers come in all shapes, sizes, and breeds!

Rita calls on the Putty Patrol when she needs warriors to fight with ferocious venom. These empty-headed clay creatures exist only to serve the Mistress of Mayhem.

When called upon, the putties appear instantly from a ball of clay. They aren't very bright — but there are certainly a lot of them.

In order to morph into Power Rangers, the teenagers must call upon the powers of the ancient dinosaurs.

Each Power Ranger controls a single Dinozord. The individual Zords are powerful, but not undefeatable. However, no one can beat the Zords when they join together to become the mighty Megazord!!

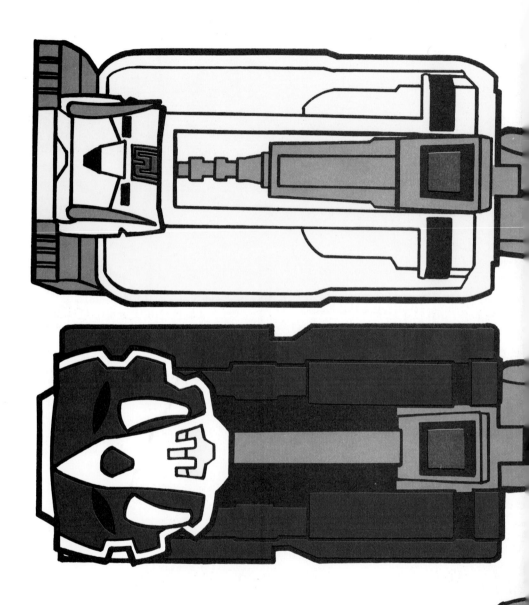

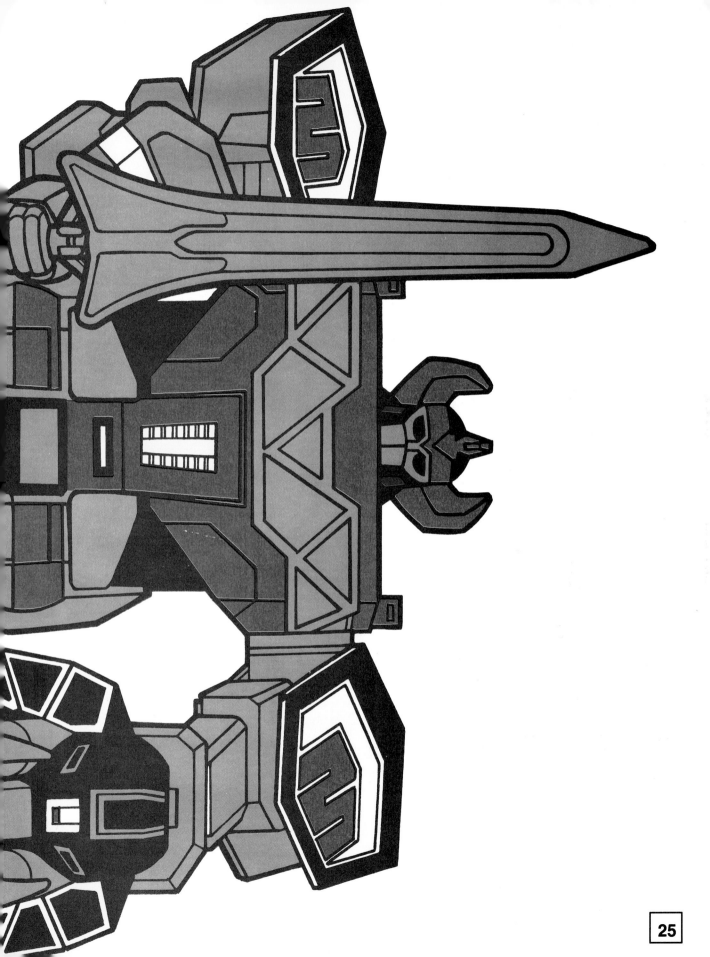

The Mighty Morphin Power Rangers are ready to do battle!

Of course, not all of the Power Rangers' troubles come from members of Rita's team. Much of it comes from regular kids, like Bulk and Skull.

Perhaps you wouldn't call Bulk and Skull "regular." They are the kind of kids who are used to getting D's in school — D for detention, that is! Whether they are starting a food fight, dressing in costumes, or trying to steal Billy's exam notes, it doesn't take much thinking or power to outsmart these two.

So, for most of their days, the Power Rangers can enjoy their time like any other teenagers. But they can never completely relax. They know there will always come a time when they will be called upon to morph into Power Rangers – and save us all from Rita Repulsa.

Go, go, Power Rangers!!